W9-AVL-902

J

S

What Freedom Means to Me

A Flag Day Story

Written and Illustrated
by
Heather French Henry

Cubbie Blue Publishing
Woodland Hills, California

Design by Jaye Oliver

Published by Cubbie Blue Publishing
21900 Marylee Street, #290, Woodland Hills, CA 91367

Printed in the United States of America

Publisher's Cataloging-in-Publication Data

Henry, Heather French.

　　What freedom means to me : a Flag Day story / written and illustrated by Heather French Henry. -- Woodland Hills, CA : Cubbie Blue Publishing, 2004.

　　　　p. ; cm.
　　　　(Claire's holiday adventures)

　　　　Audience: ages 4-10.
　　　　Summary: General Jones teaches Claire and Robbie that freedom comes with responsibility and means different things to different people. Brief history of the origin of the flag (with Betsy Ross) is included.

　　　　ISBN: 0-9706341-2-9
　　　　0-9706341-9-6 (pbk.)

　　　　1. Flag Day--Juvenile fiction. 2. Liberty--Juvenile fiction. 3. Flags--United States--Juvenile fiction. I. Title. II. Series.

PZ7.H467 W43 2004　　　　2003114801
[E]--dc22　　　　0406

10 9 8 7 6 5 4 3 2 1

"Come here, Pepper," ordered Claire. But Pepper had other plans. She dashed next door and began barking at the neighbor's cat.

Claire ran after her, leash in hand and her best friend Robbie at her heels.

The eight year old finally hitched the leash to her puppy's collar.

"Pepper doesn't obey very well," observed her neighbor, General Jones.

"She never listens," Claire sputtered. "Sometimes it gets her in trouble."

"Pepper's still a pup. She'll learn to listen," advised General Jones.

Pepper tugged on the leash. "I hate ordering her around. I'm sure she hates it, too," Claire sighed.

"Maybe she'd enjoy celebrating Flag Day with us," said the general. "Come, let's raise our country's very first flag."

"Cool," said Claire, tightening her hold on Pepper's leash. "But then I have to go clean my room."

General Jones removed a large flag from its box.
"Why's it folded into a triangle?" Robbie asked.
"To look like the hats the first patriots wore in their fight for freedom," said the general.

As they prepared to raise the flag, Claire frowned. "It's not the real one," she wailed. "It's missing too many stars."

"What happened to them?" Robbie asked.

"They showed up later," explained General Jones. "The first flag, made by Betsy Ross, had thirteen stars—one for each colony that broke free from the British." Reaching back into the box, he took out art supplies and poster-board stars.

"Let's make our own Betsy Ross flag!" beamed Claire. She tied Pepper under the table then reached for the scissors.

The general chuckled. "My kids made one every year when they were young. That's why there's more than a flag in this box."

"We could write on these stars," said Claire, holding up two of the stars they had cut out.

"Yeah," said Robbie. "We could write what freedom means to different people."

"Okay, I'll start," declared the general. He wrote, "Living like a patriot."

Does Pepper live like a patriot? Claire wondered.

General Jones removed fabric from the
box and draped it across the table. Claire and
Robbie agreed to go fill out stars and come
back to make their flag before sunset.
Pepper was invited, too.

On her way home, Claire chased down the mail carrier. "What does freedom mean to you?" she asked, panting.

"Delivering mail by day and studying law at night," he replied.

"Acting silly sometimes," said a girl buzzing by like a bumblebee. "At least I'm not a dog. Dogs aren't free."

But they were born free, Claire thought to herself.

When she got home, Claire printed each answer on a star. Then she handed her mom a blank one.

Mom wrote, "Being true to myself."

Can Pepper be true to herself? Claire mused.

"Why so sad?" asked Mom as Claire snuggled outside with her puppy.

"I'm sure Pepper doesn't feel free," Claire said.

"She looks happy to me," suggested Mom. "By the way, did you clean your room?"

"I will, Mom," replied Claire, racing Pepper around the yard.

At Robbie's house, his dad wrote, "Voting for leaders who represent the people."

Robbie's sister scribbled, "Being elected president and always speaking my mind."

His grandmother penned, "Changing as gracefully as the seasons."

Claire and Robbie returned with their stars and got right to work. Pepper did too, pouncing on the glue and leaving sticky paw-prints everywhere.

"Stop," Claire shouted. Groaning, she tied her pup under the table again.

"I see lots of freedom stars," said the general, "but none for the two of you."

Claire reached for a star and wrote, "Not worrying about Pepper."

On his, Robbie scrawled, "Not being a slave."

"Hmm, we're still missing Pepper's," the general pointed out.

"She doesn't *have* freedom," Claire balked.

"Because Claire's like that nasty British king who ordered the first Americans around," teased Robbie.

Claire pouted, thinking about her own orders and her mom's. "Are we still free when we do what we're told?" she asked the general.
He smiled. "Following guidelines doesn't erase freedom."

Pepper lunged toward the cat, tugging at her leash.

"Pepper will never be totally free, but I will because I won't have to listen to grown-ups," said Claire.

"Not quite," the general replied. "There will always be traffic lights to obey."

"Then obeying isn't like being a slave?" asked Robbie, in disbelief.

"Not when it makes life safer for everyone," the general told him.

"I get it," Claire blurted out, grabbing the final star. "Some things—like moms and traffic lights and good leaders—guide us to a safe freedom. That's just what the patriots discovered!"

"Let's see . . . I'm free and so is Pepper. And I'm not a monster," she said, glaring at Robbie. She filled in Pepper's star and handed it to the general. Then she glued her own star to the flag.

As General Jones glued Pepper's star in place, his eyes danced with laughter. He read the words aloud: "Obeying Claire."

Robbie and Claire held up their creation. "Our Betsy Ross flag is complete. I salute everyone's freedom star, especially Pepper's," said Robbie.

"And I'll try not to get mad when she disobeys," vowed Claire.

"It's already sunset," said the general. "Time to take down the flag honoring the early patriots..."

"Who proved they were ready to follow good leaders," Claire added, without skipping a beat.

"Claire!" Mom called from across the yard.

"Oops, I forgot to clean my room," gasped Claire. "I guess I'm a little like Pepper. We both forget to obey." She hurried home with her puppy.

"Freedom is tricky, Pepper," Claire mumbled while putting her toys away. "I hate chores like you hate your leash—but obeying makes us safe and free."

The smell of chocolate chip cookies, just starting to bake, floated up the stairs and into Claire's room. "Obeying also makes us happy," she said, hugging her puppy. "I think we're beginning patriots."

A Brief History of Flag Day

George Washington is said to have visited Betsy Ross, a Philadelphia seamstress, in June 1776, showing her a rough design for a flag of the United States. On June 14, 1777, the Continental Congress voted that the first flag would have thirteen alternating red and white stripes and that the union of the thirteen colonies be represented by thirteen white stars on a blue field, symbolizing a new constellation. From among the many designs submitted by flag-makers, Congress adopted one by Betsy Ross that displayed the stars in a circle. Beginning in July 1818, a new star was added for each state that joined the union. Nearly one hundred years later, in 1916, President Woodrow Wilson declared June 14 as Flag Day.

Today's flag, still with thirteen red and white stripes, has fifty white stars arranged in rows on a blue field. The red stands for courage, the white for innocence, and the blue for justice.